CLASSIC STARTS™

The Last of
the Mohicans

*Retold from the James Fenimore Cooper
original by Deanna McFadden*

Illustrated by Troy Howell

STERLING

New York / London
www.sterlingpublishing.com/kids

STERLING and the distinctive Sterling logo
are registered trademarks of Sterling Publishing Co., Inc.

Library of Congress Cataloging-in-Publication Data

McFadden, Deanna.
 The last of the Mohicans / retold from the James Fenimore Cooper original;
abridged by Deanna McFadden; illustrated by Troy Howell; afterword by
Arthur Pober.
  p. cm. — (Classic starts)
 Summary: An abridged version of the novel chronicling a Mohican brave's
struggle to protect two English girls from an evil Huron during the French and
Indian War.
 ISBN-13: 978-1-4027-4577-5 (alk. paper)
 ISBN-10: 1-4027-4577-X (alk. paper)
 1. United States—History—French and Indian War, 1755–1763—Juvenile
fiction. 2. Mohegan Indians—Juvenile fiction. [1. United States—History—
French and Indian War, 1755–1763—Fiction. 2. Mohegan Indians—Fiction.
3. Indians of North America—East (U.S.)—Fiction.] I. Howell, Troy, ill.
II. Cooper, James Fenimore, 1789–1851. Last of the Mohicans. III. Title.

PZ7.M4784548Las 2008
[Fic]—dc22

                                                                    2007003949

2 4 6 8 10 9 7 5 3 1

Published by Sterling Publishing Co., Inc.
387 Park Avenue South, New York, NY 10016
Copyright © 2008 by Deanna McFadden
Illustrations copyright © 2008 by Troy Howell
Distributed in Canada by Sterling Publishing
c/*o* Canadian Manda Group, 165 Dufferin Street,
Toronto, Ontario, Canada M6K 3H6
Distributed in the United Kingdom by GMC Distribution Services,
Castle Place, 166 High Street, Lewes, East Sussex, England BN7 1XU
Distributed in Australia by Capricorn Link (Australia) Pty. Ltd.
P.O. Box 704, Windsor, NSW 2756, Australia

Classic Starts is a trademark of Sterling Publishing Co., Inc.

Printed in China
All rights reserved

Sterling ISBN-13: 978-1-4027-4577-5
ISBN-10: 1-4027-4577-X

For information about custom editions, special sales, premium and
corporate purchases, please contact Sterling Special Sales
Department at 800-805-5489 or specialsales@sterlingpublishing.com.

CONTENTS

*

CHAPTER 1

The Battleground

This story takes place in the third year of the last war between the French and the English. The two countries were fighting over the land that would become Canada and the United States. Forts were set up and fought over as farmers fled the battle-grounds. It was a terrible war, particularly during the cold winter months, and the troops were happy to see summer arrive.

The sound of war drums in the middle of the night awoke the tired, worn-out English soldiers of Fort Edward. They knew at once that the

French commander, Montcalm, was coming up the river with a large army. Their leader, General Webb, ordered his fifteen hundred soldiers to march up the river at dawn to meet the French army at Fort William Henry.

At first light, the soldiers rode out on their strong horses. Great big wagons carrying supplies followed, kicking up dust as they went.

Inside General Webb's house, Cora and Alice Munro—the daughters of the general who was in charge of Fort William Henry—were preparing for their journey home. Outside, Major Duncan Heyward was making sure that everything was ready for the trip. An Indian scout named Magua stood beside him.

With Montcalm coming up the river to attack the English, the journey back to Fort William Henry would be very dangerous. Duncan and Magua were to make sure that the girls made it home safely.

The thought of Alice's safety weighed heavily on Duncan's mind as he tightened the horses' saddles. He had strong feelings for General Munro's beautiful young daughter, and did not wish to see her harmed in any way.

As they were getting the horses ready, a tall, thin man walked up to Duncan and Magua. He wore a large hat and carried a pitch pipe.

He said to Duncan, "This is a beautiful horse— I saw many of them at New Haven. He's perfect looking, isn't he?"

Duncan looked at the man strangely and carried on with his preparations. The stranger stood there for a while waiting for an answer, but when none came, he walked away.

A few minutes later, the cabin door opened and the sisters came out. Alice, the younger of the two, was very fair. She had blond hair and blue eyes, and was quite beautiful. Duncan helped her up on her horse. He smiled kindly at

her, and blushed a little when she thanked him for his hand.

Then he turned and helped Cora onto her own horse. General Webb came out to say good-bye. The three nodded farewell to him as they rode away.

Just as Duncan and the girls were leaving the camp, Magua shot past them on his horse. The quick movement startled Alice, who let out a sharp, "Oh my!"

Cora's fiery eyes stared straight ahead, and she didn't flinch. Instead, she calmly pulled her veil down so it covered her dark brown hair and eyes.

CHAPTER 2

The Path

‿∾

Alice laughed at her own fright, and said to Duncan, "For a minute, I thought he might be a ghost! I'll have to be braver, like a true Munro, if we're to run into Montcalm."

"Magua knows his way around Lake George. If we are to get back to Fort William Henry safely, he's the one to guide us. There will be no chance of us running into Montcalm," Duncan said.

"Do you know Magua well?" Alice asked, "I mean, do you trust him?"

"I do know him," Duncan said. "And I do trust

him. He is said to be a great Indian scout. He
ended up at our camp somewhat by accident,
although I don't know the whole story. I believe
your father had something to do with it. In the
end, it is enough that he is our friend."

"I think I would not be so scared of him if I
could hear him speak. Will you talk to him,
Duncan?" Alice asked.

"Ah, Magua rarely speaks. But he does know
the way. There is no need to be afraid. Look, he's
stopped."

Indeed, Magua had stopped in front of them.
He pointed to a thicket that stood beside the military road and said, "This is the way." The path
was dense with trees and bushes.

"What do you think, Cora?" Alice asked.
"Would we not be just as safe going the way the
soldiers did this morning? Should we not stick to
the road?"

But Cora answered, "If the French have

reached the road at all, we would be in danger. It might be best to go the way Magua suggests, so that our travels stay secret. The last thing we want is for the daughters of an English general to fall into French hands!"

She kicked her heels and pulled her horse's reins to move forward through the thicket and follow the guide. Alice went next, and then Duncan.

The trail was difficult, and it was hard to talk. Suddenly they heard a horse approaching! The small party stopped. They saw a very tall man riding a very small colt. It was the same fellow who had tried to talk to Duncan and Magua at the fort!

"You are no messenger," Duncan shouted. "I trust you to bring no ill will."

"I heard you were going to Fort William Henry," the man said. "I, too, am on my way there and thought we could go together. You could use my good company."

"You have not asked if we *need* your good company," Duncan replied.

"I thought about it a great deal," the man said. "And, well, you do."

"The way to the lake is the other direction," Duncan said coldly.

"Yes, I do know that way to the fort. But I heard the soldiers ride out this morning, and I do not want to run into the French. I know you have the same goal. And you look like you know a secret way, so here I am."

Duncan did not know whether to laugh at this fellow or to give in to his growing anger. "Who are you? What is your name?"

"I am a master of the art of singing," the man said proudly. "My name is David Gamut."

"I do not think we are in need of a song," Duncan said, "We should be quiet for—"

"Oh, Duncan," Alice interrupted, "do not frown. Let him come with us."

Duncan looked at Alice for some time, and then finally gave in, for he could never say no to someone so dear to his heart. As the group continued along the path, Cora and Duncan started talking about how long it might take to reach the fort, while Alice politely asked David about his work. Instantly, the music instructor started to sing at the top of his voice.

"It would be best if we are quiet as we make our way through the forest," Duncan said. "Pardon me, Alice, for I know you are enjoying the song, but it's not safe."

"But it's so pretty!" Alice replied.

"The safety of you and Cora is all I care about. If you don't mind, sir, the singing must cease."

CHAPTER 3

Hawkeye and the Last Mohican

∝

A few miles away, two men sat talking beside a small stream deep in the forest. One, a strong, dark-haired man, sat on a mossy log. His name was Hawkeye. He wore an old, dark green hunting shirt and gray moccasins on his feet. In his belt he carried a sharp hunting knife. His rifle rested against a tree next to him.

He and Chingachgook, the chief of the Mohican tribe, were deep in conversation about how quickly the world around them was changing.

"My son, Uncas, is the last of our kind," Chingachgook said. "He is the last of the Mohicans. When he is gone, our tribe will exist no more."

At that moment, a young warrior raced between the two men and sat down beside Chingachgook.

"Here I am," Uncas said. "What are you discussing?"

"Hawkeye and I were talking about the past and the future," Chingachgook answered.

The young warrior fell to the ground and listened. "I hear horses," he said.

"Perhaps it is wolves," Hawkeye suggested.

"No," Uncas answered. "They are your people, the English, from the fort. You must go speak to them."

"I would if I heard anything!" Hawkeye said and smiled. "But I can't hear a single hoof!"

Uncas motioned for him to be quiet. A dry stick cracked.

"There," Hawkeye whispered. "I mistook them for the waterfalls. I hear them now. For their own good, I hope the Hurons can't hear them. I should go and warn them that the woods are not safe."

But before Hawkeye could set out to find the men on horses, Duncan and the girls appeared before him.

"Who are you?" Hawkeye asked. "What are you doing in this part of the forest?"

"I am a soldier, charged with taking these girls to Fort William Henry," Duncan said. "We've been traveling most of the day."

"Are you lost?" Hawkeye asked.

"I believe we are. Do you know how far we are from the fort?" Duncan asked.

Hawkeye laughed, and then grew quiet, afraid that the Hurons might hear him. "You are going in the wrong direction. You'd be better off heading to Fort Edward, where the army is, and speaking with General Webb. He's in charge there."

David came up beside them and said, "We left Fort Edward this morning. How far are we from Fort William Henry?"

"You must have lost your eyesight before you lost your way," Hawkeye replied. "There's a road that takes you right to Fort William Henry."

"It is an excellent road," Duncan replied. "But to stay away from the French and to be safe, we hired an Indian guide, Magua, to show us a different way. Now we are lost."

Hawkeye looked at the soldier. "An Indian, lost in the woods? That seems strange. Is he a Mohawk?"

"I think he was born to the North. A Huron, perhaps?"

At that, Chingachgook and Uncas rose and stood beside Hawkeye. "It sounds as if you shouldn't have trusted this scout," Hawkeye said.

"Oh, don't be silly. He is our friend, of that I am sure. Now—how far to Fort William Henry? We could reward you well to take us there. I am Major Duncan Heyward, and these are General Munro's daughters, who are trying to get home." He pointed to Cora and Alice, who were waiting patiently for him.

Hawkeye looked surprised. "Yes, I heard a party was leaving this morning for Fort William

Henry. I am the scout Hawkeye. It seems strange to me that your guide would desert you."

"I think he has gone too far ahead," Duncan said.

"Fort William Henry is just an hour's ride from here," Hawkeye said. "I can show you, but it is a rough ride, not meant for women."

Cora and Alice did not hear him say this, or they would have protested. Instead, Duncan told Hawkeye that although they were tired, they could certainly ride for another hour. Then he whispered, "I started to suspect our guide was leading us astray, so I sent him ahead. But now I am convinced that he will not return."

"You wait here. We'll soon find him—and the truth." Then Hawkeye stepped away to speak with Chingachgook and Uncas, and the three of them took off into the forest.

CHAPTER 4

A Secret Hideaway

Duncan stayed behind with the girls and David for a moment, but then decided that he should help chase down the missing scout.

"Cora, Alice," he said, "You'll be safe here with David. I'm going to find Hawkeye and see what's going on."

"Oh, Duncan," Alice said, "Do you really think Magua has abandoned us?"

"Everything will be fine, my dear. You know I would never let anything happen to you or your sister."

Alice smiled, and Cora said, "We'll be fine. We're strong. We're Munros! Good luck!"

Duncan had gone only a hundred yards when he found Hawkeye, Chingachgook, and Uncas. They were standing with their heads together.

"What happened?" Duncan asked.

"He slipped away from us," Hawkeye replied.

"Well, let's go! We can find him. There are four of us now and only one of him."

"Ah," Hawkeye said, "but he could just as easily call others to fight with him. We need to get moving so he doesn't find us so easily."

Duncan looked up and saw the clouds thinning. Day was beginning to turn into night. He wanted to get Hawkeye's attention, but the scout was speaking to Chingachgook and Uncas in Delaware, the language of their people. The three men started to walk away.

"Wait!" Duncan said. "Where are you going?"

The men stopped and spoke to one another

again. After a few minutes, Hawkeye turned to Duncan and said, "Uncas is right. We cannot leave you lost in the forest and at the mercy of your guide."

"I've already told you—we'll pay anything," Duncan said.

Hawkeye looked at him. "We don't want your money. We'll help you because it is the right thing to do. But you must promise two things."

"Yes," Duncan said. "Of course we will."

"One, you must be as still as the woods and let what is going to happen, happen. Two, you must keep the place we are going to take you a secret."

Duncan nodded. "Fine, let's go—we have little time to spare before the sun sets completely."

The four men walked back to where David was waiting with Alice and Cora. Duncan quickly told them what had happened to the guide, and then helped the women down off their horses. He explained to them that Magua had betrayed them and might be trying to hurt them. They had to go with these men, the Mohicans and Hawkeye.

Cora and Alice trusted Duncan's word and went with him. David followed along behind them. They met Hawkeye and the Mohicans down by the water's edge.

"We must let the horses go," Hawkeye said. "If Magua and his men see them grazing by the riverbanks, they will assume you have made your camp nearby. Our only chance to escape is to go on foot."

The sisters held each other's hands to hide their fear, while Duncan carefully searched the surrounding woods. Hawkeye took the bridles off the horses and set the animals free. Then he started to walk away. The small group followed.

A short distance from the glen, they walked under a waterfall and came out the other side. Hawkeye uncovered two canoes from the brush.

He signaled for Cora and Alice to step into one, and then joined them. Duncan, David, Chingachgook, and Uncas stepped into the other canoe. As they paddled along, Hawkeye listened to every sound the forest made.

The river started to move quickly. Alice and Cora were afraid they would be dashed against the rocks, but Hawkeye and the Mohicans were good paddlers. The group soon came to a rocky section of the river and Hawkeye stopped the canoe.

"Stay here," Hawkeye told the travelers. "We will go and make sure we're safe."

Hawkeye, Chingachgook, and Uncas left the party standing on the rocks. They didn't have long to wait before the men returned.

"Quickly now," Hawkeye said. He hid the canoes under some brush, and then disappeared into the face of a rock.

CHAPTER 5

A Safe Haven?

Hidden in the side of the rocks was an entrance to a series of caves. Hawkeye motioned for everyone to walk inside. Once they were all within the safety of the rocky walls, Hawkeye and Uncas went back outside to stand guard.

"Do you think we are safe now, Duncan?" Alice asked.

Before Duncan could answer, Hawkeye said "The fire grows too bright, Uncas. Drop the blanket to the cave."

"Are we quite safe?" Duncan shouted "Is there no danger of surprise?"

A figure moved at the back of the cave. The girls shouted in fright, but it was only Chingachgook, showing them the other entrance to the cavern.

"See," Hawkeye said as he came toward the back. "There is another way out. You'll be quite safe here."

Duncan looked around. "Are we on some sort of island?" he asked.

"We're between two waterfalls," Hawkeye answered. "The river is both above and below."

While the group made a rough dinner of deer meat, Uncas did his best to make sure that Cora and Alice were comfortable. Chingachgook sat apart from the group and watched everything carefully.

"Now," Hawkeye said to the musician. "I do not know who you are."

"My name is David Gamut," the musician answered.

"Tell me, what do you do?"

"I teach singing," David replied.

"That's a strange kind of job. Why don't you sing a little now? It will make the girls feel better."

David started to sing quietly, and Cora and Alice joined in.

Suddenly a strange cry stopped the singing. Everyone fell silent.

"What was that?" Alice whispered.

No one replied. Hawkeye spoke to the two Mohicans, and then Uncas quietly left the cave.

"We don't know what made that noise," Hawkeye said. "It's like nothing we have ever heard before in this forest."

"Is it not a sound that warriors make before battle?" Cora asked.

"If you had ever heard a warrior cry,"

Hawkeye said, "you would never mistake it for *that* sound."

Uncas came back inside.

"Can you see the fire from outside?" Hawkeye asked him. Uncas shook his head.

"We're safe, then," Hawkeye told the girls. He gestured to the second cave and said, "Cora, Alice, please go and get some sleep. We'll need to travel most of tomorrow. You need your rest."

Cora stood up and did as she was told. Alice also stood, but before she made her way farther into the cave, she asked Duncan to come with them. "Please don't leave us alone," she said. "That terrible cry has scared me to death."

"Let us first look around the cave and make sure it's safe." Duncan took a torch from the fire and shone it in every direction, looking around carefully. "Good men are guarding the front. There is no way anyone can get through the back without us hearing them. I assure you, girls, you are quite safe."

"I imagine Father is very worried about us," Alice cried softly.

"Alice," Cora said, "you need to be brave. I am the older sister. Follow my example."

"And he is a soldier, your father," Duncan added. "He knows I am with you, and will keep you safe. That is my duty."

"But he is still our father," Alice said. "And I am sure he's worried."

Before either could say another word, the same loud, piercing cry filled the air. Hawkeye lifted up the blanket to the entrance and looked at the three of them. The girls shivered. Even Duncan's brave face seemed to falter.

There was some kind of danger afoot and even a man of the woods like Hawkeye wasn't entirely sure what might happen.

CHAPTER 6

The Sound Explained

༄

"You two should stay here," Hawkeye said to the girls. "Duncan can come outside and watch the woods with us."

"Are we in much danger?" Cora asked.

"The one that made that sound is the only one who knows," Hawkeye answered.

"What if it was not a man, but a ghost? Or maybe our enemies are making the awful sound just to scare us," Cora said.

"No man-made sound can trick me. I know

the sounds of these woods like I know my own voice. And yet neither the Mohicans nor I can explain that noise."

Duncan said, "It is extraordinary. Come, let's go and see what it could be."

"We're going with you," Cora said, as she pulled Alice along behind her.

"I insist you both stay here," Duncan said. "I am responsible for your safety, and I doubt your father would like it if I let you go out into the woods without knowing what made that noise."

"But Duncan," Cora said, "would we not be safer with you and Hawkeye?"

"Perhaps she is right," Hawkeye said. "Come, we shall go as a group."

A heavy breeze blew across the evening. The air was cool, and it did everyone good to be outside. It was a still night. The streams and waterfalls were the only things moving in the forest. Every pair of eyes was looking toward the shore, trying to see if they could make out the source of the terrible noise.

"There's nothing here but the stream," Duncan said. "How we would love a night like this if it weren't for that sound. I wonder . . ."

"Shhh!" Alice said. "Listen."

Sure enough, the sound arose once more.

"Show yourself!" Hawkeye shouted. "Show yourself now!"

"Wait!" Duncan said, "I know that sound. It's the sound a horse makes when it's in trouble. I didn't recognize it before because it was echoing off the walls of the caves. I've heard it on the battlefield. One of the horses must be caught in something."

Hawkeye spoke to Uncas and asked him to go check on the horses.

"Make camp over there, under that tree," Hawkeye told the rest of the group. "We'll wait here for the first light of day."

Hawkeye's worry had disappeared, now that the noise had been explained. Uncas returned and told him that one of the horses had indeed caught its hoof on a root.

The sisters laid down close to each other and fell right asleep. Hours went by. David and Duncan slept as well. Hawkeye, Chingachgook, and Uncas stayed awake, carefully watching the row of trees.

Finally, a pale streak of light began to show itself. Hawkeye stood and shook Duncan. "Wake up Cora and Alice. Get them ready and meet us at the shore. I'll bring the canoes."

"Sleep must have gotten the best of me," Duncan said. "I did try to stay awake."

"We still have some darkness left. Be quick, and be quiet."

Duncan lifted up the shawl that lay across Cora and Alice. Cora raised up her hand as if to stop him, and Alice mumbled in her sleep, "No, no, Father. Duncan was with us. We were not deserted."

Duncan smiled, and then whispered, "Cora, Alice, time to wake."

Suddenly there were terrible whoops and cries all around them. Cora sat up quickly, and Alice screamed.

David stood up and said, "What on earth could that be?"

A shot rang out. It whizzed by and grazed David's ear. Luckily, Duncan caught him before he fell and pulled David and the girls back into the cave. "Stay here where it's safe."

Hawkeye came running toward them and said, "He's lucky to be alive."

"Will he be okay?" Cora asked.

"Stay here with him," Hawkeye replied. "We'll be back as soon as we can. If you have a handkerchief, press it against his ear. He should wake up shortly. He wasn't hit very hard."

Cora pulled her kerchief from her waistband and did as she was told.

They could hear shouts, whoops, and calls from the woods.

Hawkeye raced off to join Uncas and Chingachgook, who were fending off their attackers. Duncan waited for David to stir. Then he, too, got up and followed the other men.

"Duncan," Alice said. "Don't go."

He smiled kindly at her, happy for her concern. "It is my duty," he said. "There are at least forty men out there and I need to help Hawkeye. I'll be all right, I promise."

Duncan slipped outside and bent down beside Hawkeye on the rocks in front of the caves. The two men watched as their enemies positioned themselves across the river. Members of the enemy tribe tried to cross the water, but the current was too strong. One warrior was sucked right under. Duncan almost stood up to try and help him.

"Wait," Hawkeye whispered, "you'll give us away if you leave now."

Hawkeye whistled, and Uncas appeared beside them. At the same moment, four men, including Magua, leaped out of the woods. They were still yards away, but their cries echoed out into the sky. Hawkeye and Uncas waited patiently for them to get closer.

When they finally did, a great fight took place. Sharp yells and quick shouts were heard. Hands and fists flew. Duncan fought with all of his might. Slowly, the enemies fell.

"Hurry!" Hawkeye shouted. "Run back to the caves."

Uncas whooped and followed Duncan and Hawkeye back into the shelter of the rocks.

CHAPTER 7

A Shot from a Tree

David was the only one injured in the fight. Chingachgook remained at his post while Hawkeye laid on the ground in a safe, secluded place and watched the woods carefully. Shots could be heard in the distance. Uncas stood on guard.

"Let them waste their bullets!" Hawkeye shouted. "We know we are safe." He laughed.

Duncan lay beside Hawkeye. "I owe Uncas a great debt. Just as I left the caves, I was caught off guard by one of our enemies. Uncas pulled me out of the way. He saved my life."

Suddenly, Uncas appeared next to them. He clapped Duncan on the back, and said, "Friends?"

Duncan nodded. "Of course!"

Just then, a shot hit a rock beside them and Duncan jumped. Uncas put his hand over his mouth, indicating that they should be quiet. He pointed to an oak tree where one of their enemies was sitting and trying to hide.

"Come, Uncas. We must be quick," Hawkeye whispered.

Hawkeye and Uncas swiftly stood up and left the safety of their hiding place. Chingachgook joined them, and the three sped away toward the oak. The fighting continued until the man fell out of the tree.

Afterward, Hawkeye said, "Uncas, make your way down to the canoes. We need more powder and supplies."

Hawkeye shook out his powder horn and pouch to make sure they were indeed empty, and the young Mohican raced off. Seconds later, Duncan and Hawkeye heard him shout—a signal of some new danger. They ran down the hill to see what was happening. Shots flew all around them. More of Magua's men had returned to fight!

Uncas's cry brought Cora, Alice, and David down to the water's edge as well. The group watched as their canoe drifted by. One of their enemies had found it hidden in the bushes and pushed it into the river.

"It's too late!" Hawkeye shouted, "It's all lost. All of our powder, all of our supplies."

The Huron scout shouted his victory across the river.

"What can we do?" Duncan asked. "What will become of us?"

Hawkeye's face grew angry when he heard the

Hurons across the river laughing at him, but he said nothing.

"Surely our case is not so desperate!" David insisted. "We can still fight!"

Chingachgook took off his tomahawk and his eagle feather in defeat.

Cora looked at the men and said, "Why must we all die? Take to the woods. Go, we owe you too much already."

"And leave you here? We could never do that," Hawkeye answered. "Besides, there is no safe way out of the woods."

"Then you must take to the river. Why stay behind and let them hurt more people?" Cora asked.

"What would we tell your father, Cora?" Hawkeye said sharply. "What should we say when he asks us why we abandoned his daughters?"

"You must go to him. Tell him we are here, about to be attacked by the Hurons, but that we've fled into the northern woods. Tell him that his men can rescue us if they hurry."

Hawkeye spoke to Chingachgook and Uncas. The elder Mohican listened carefully. After a moment, he waved his hands and said, "Good." He put his tomahawk back on his belt and his eagle feather back on his head. Chingachgook nodded to Uncas and Hawkeye, and then sped to the edge of the rocks and dropped into the water.

Hawkeye looked at Cora. "You are very brave," he said. "If they do take you away, break small sticks along your path—that way we'll be able to find you."

Then he turned and went the same way as Chingachgook. Only Uncas remained.

"I will stay," he said in English. "It is not right to leave you here to your fate."

"No," Cora said. "Please go and find my father. We are well hidden here, and will remain so until you return."

Uncas looked unhappy for a moment, but then did as Cora asked. He, too, stood on the edge of the rocks and jumped into the water. After one last look at Uncas, Cora turned to Duncan and said, "I know you can swim well, Duncan. It's your turn now."

"It is my duty to protect you. And, I——" he stammered, "I can't leave Alice behind."

"And you have done a good job. Now we need you to go and find our father. The worst they'll do is capture us. If you're here, they might kill us. You know I'm right! Please, Duncan, I will protect Alice."

Duncan didn't say anything. He looked at the beautiful Alice and did not want to leave. "There are evils worse than being captured," he said. "I am not leaving you behind."

After Hawkeye and the Mohicans left, Duncan stood watch outside the caves, while Cora and Alice tucked themselves inside. The only thing Duncan could hear was the rush of the water. The forest seemed absent even of animal life. The river banks looked deserted. Duncan could neither see nor hear any of the enemies in the distance, but he did not doubt that they were there.

Duncan stepped inside and saw David resting near the front of the caves. "The Hurons are nowhere to be seen. But we should remain hidden for now," he said.

"My head is quite sore," David replied. "I am somewhat thankful for the rest."

"We must put up the blankets," Duncan said. "Are you strong enough? Then we should go to Alice and Cora."

The two men lifted up the blankets and hung them exactly as the Mohicans had. Now if they lit a fire, no one would be able to see the light from outside.

David leaned on Duncan as they made their way to the back of the cave. There was a bed of sassafras in the cave, and David happily laid on top of it, pulling some blankets over himself to keep warm.

Duncan looked to Cora and said, "Where life remains, there is hope." Then he looked at Alice, who was crying.

She wiped her eyes and said, "There. I am calmer now, Duncan. Surely we are safe in this hidden spot."

Duncan knelt by her and squeezed her hand. "With two brave souls like you and Cora behind me, I feel no fear." Then he went toward the front of the cave to keep watch.

David played a tune on his pitch pipe and began to sing.

Cora whispered, "Might the singing be dangerous?"

"The sound of the waterfalls will drown out his voice," Duncan answered.

David sang and sang. Cora and Alice looked at him with kind eyes. Even Duncan could not help but smile. But the happy moment did not last long. Suddenly they heard a loud yell from outside.

"We are all caught!" Alice whispered. "It's over."

"Not just yet," Duncan said. "That sound came from the island. The waterfalls are still protecting us."

The group in the cave fell silent. Soon they could hear yells and shouts from all around them. One came so close to the entrance of the caves that Duncan thought they would be found.

"Come," he whispered. "We need to get into the smaller cave at the back. Hurry."

The girls helped David to his feet and quickly moved behind another set of hanging blankets. It was none too soon, either. The Hurons had found the front cave. They turned over the sassafras beds and whooped in delight. But they did not see the back entrance.

When they had gone, Duncan sighed. "They have left," he said. "We're safe once more. You all stay here. I'm going to see for sure."

Cora followed him. They were not yet outside the cave when she saw something that turned her face pale: Magua!

Duncan spotted him also, and he could tell that the Huron's eyes had not yet adjusted to the dark cave. Duncan fired his pistol without thinking. Magua saw him and let out a great yell. Within seconds, the cave was full of Hurons.

CHAPTER 8

A Long Journey

⌒

While the rest of the men searched the cave, the Hurons held Duncan, Cora, Alice, and David tightly.

"What are they looking for?" Duncan asked Magua.

"La Longue Carabine," he replied. "The long rifle—who you call Hawkeye. He and those he travels with are the enemies of my people."

"He is gone," Duncan said.

"Where is his body?" Magua demanded. "Where can we find it?"

"He's not dead," Duncan answered. "He escaped."

"The Mohicans, too?"

"Yes. They all swam down the river. You will not find them."

Magua turned and explained to his men what had happened to Hawkeye and the Mohicans. Some raced down to the river to see for themselves. Others hit the walls of the cave in anger.

Soon the four prisoners were pulled out of the cave and down toward the water. The men forced them into canoes and across the river. When they landed, half of the Hurons climbed on their horses and sped away to hunt Hawkeye and the Mohicans. Cora, Alice, David, and Duncan were left with Magua.

Duncan thought that they would be taken straight to Montcalm. He slowly stepped forward to speak with Magua and offered him money to take them to Fort William Henry.

"Enough!" Magua said. "You will speak only when spoken to."

Magua and his men pushed Cora and Alice into saddles on top of two horses. Duncan walked beside them as the entire party moved forward. Poor David also had to walk, even though his head still hurt.

The party walked in the opposite direction of Fort William Henry. They followed a path that wound first one way and then another. Duncan knew that it was meant to confuse them so they wouldn't be able to find Magua's camp on their own. They walked a long distance without any hope of stopping.

Cora remembered what Hawkeye had told her—to break a branch whenever she could. She reached out her slender arm and broke a twig that was within her grasp. It was hard to do because Magua's men were watching her every movement. But in one lucky moment, she was

able to drop her glove and break off a large branch.

"Wait!" Magua shouted. "I saw that!"

He quickly rode his horse over to the girls, jumped off, and picked up the glove. "There will be no more tricks like this—and no more breaking sticks, either."

Magua told one of his men to go back along the wrong path and break more branches.

They traveled all day through pine trees, rough paths, and across brooks and streams. Speedy and certain of where he was going, Magua took his horse where there was no path as easily as where there was one.

Finally they reached a meadow, and he motioned for Cora and Alice to come down off their horses. They walked up a large hill. When they got to the top, it was level and covered with trees. Magua threw himself on the ground to rest and ordered the others to do the same.

The hill was perfect for resting. They were high enough up that it would be almost impossible for someone to rescue them without Magua seeing the person first.

Duncan decided to try to talk to Magua again. "Do you not see the value in returning the girls to their father? He will reward you greatly."

"The gray-haired leader is a hard man,"

Magua said. "He is hard on his warriors. His eyes are made of stone."

"He is a strong leader, true. But he loves Cora and Alice," Duncan answered.

Magua's face had a very strange expression. Duncan did not know what to make of it.

"Tell the dark-haired one that I want to speak to her," Magua said.

Duncan didn't want to get Cora, but he did so anyway. As he led her back to where Magua stood, he whispered to her, "Offer him as much as you think your father would give for us. This could save our lives."

Cora nodded. She understood they were in great danger.

Magua looked at Duncan and said, "You. Leave."

Duncan didn't move. But then Cora said, "It's fine. Please go and see that Alice is all right."

Even though she was scared, Cora turned to

Magua and said, "What do you have to say to the daughter of General Munro?"

Magua told her a story. He said that he had fought a battle with Cora's father, but he had disobeyed the general's orders and had been punished by him. The general had hurt him very badly and made a fool of him in front of the rest of the men. Magua told Cora that he had taken her and Alice as revenge. And he intended to keep one of them forever!

"Surely it would be better to have the Munro gold than to keep us here just to have your revenge," Cora said.

But Magua just laughed as he walked away.

Suddenly two very strong men grabbed Duncan. Two others took David. They struggled and tried to fight, but Magua's men were strong and tied them to a tree. They tied up the girls as well. Alice cried as she looked at Duncan, wanting him to help her but knowing it was impossible. The men taunted and teased the girls. They poked them with sticks and laughed.

One of the men threw a tomahawk at Alice's head. It narrowly missed, and cut off a length of her hair. Duncan was so angry that he broke free of his bonds and ran to the man who had thrown the axe. They fought, and just as the man's knife was coming toward his chest, Duncan heard a *whiz* and a crack behind him.

Hawkeye, Uncas, and Chingachgook raced forward from the woods and killed the man who had fought Duncan. All around them, the Hurons began to howl and shout, shocked to see one of their men fall. A great fight broke out and, fist against fist, the two groups fought one another. Duncan battled alongside Hawkeye, Uncas, and Chingachgook.

Cora narrowly escaped death when a tomahawk grazed her shoulder. It cut the twines that bound her to the tree, and she rushed over to free Alice. Cora pulled at the ropes with all her might, but she could not break them. She sank to her knees beside her sister.

All of Magua's men had fallen except the leader himself. He was locked in a battle with Chingachgook. They rolled toward the high edge of the hill. With one last ounce of strength, Chingachgook pushed Magua over.

Uncas and Duncan rushed over to the girls and freed Alice, who fell into Cora's arms.

Hawkeye was still shouting victory when they noticed that Magua had not fallen to his death after all. He raced down the hill and away from the Mohicans. Uncas and Chingachgook started running after him.

"No!" Hawkeye shouted, "He's just one man with no weapons. What can he do?"

Although they didn't want to let Magua go, Uncas and Chingachgook knew Hawkeye was right. They stopped chasing Magua and returned to the group.

"We are free!" Alice exclaimed happily. "And even dear Duncan has escaped without harm."

Suddenly they realized that David was still tied up. Hawkeye cut him free, while Duncan and Uncas helped the girls to their feet. Then they all made their way down the hill to where Magua's horses were grazing.

Cora and Alice rode while the rest walked. Soon they crossed a stream and came to a dell shaded by elm trees. There they passed around a gourd of water and prepared some food.

When they were all seated, Duncan asked, "How did you find us? And how did you save us with no help from the soldiers?"

Hawkeye laughed. "If we had waited for the soldiers, we couldn't have saved you. We hid by the river and watched the Hurons."

"Then you saw everything!" Duncan said.

"Not everything," Hawkeye answered. "We were hiding. But we heard the whole thing. We followed your tracks by marking the footprints of the horses.

"It was hard to keep Uncas from rushing right in to save everyone. We had to wait for the right moment—until we knew we had the advantage of surprise."

As he was speaking, Hawkeye offered the drinking gourd to Duncan, who took a long sip. When they finished eating, Hawkeye said it was time to go. Cora and Alice took one last look around the beautiful spring and then climbed atop their horses. The whole party moved quickly toward the north on a narrow path.

CHAPTER 9

Ghosts in the Forest

ℭ∽

Hawkeye covered their tracks to make it harder for Magua to find them. After they had been walking for a long time, he moved aside some large tree branches and cut a path through a briar bush. Then he led them to an old cabin. The roof had all but fallen in, but the walls were sound. Cora and Alice hesitantly stepped down from their horses, afraid of going inside such a rundown place.

"Wouldn't it be better if we stayed hidden in the woods?" Duncan asked.

"Oh, very few know of this house. We are safe here," Hawkeye answered, and told the group about a great battle that had been fought there years ago.

When Cora and Alice heard the story, they were afraid to sit on a field where such a battle had been fought, but Hawkeye assured them that there was no chance the ghosts would bother them!

Then the Mohicans and Hawkeye got to work. They made beds for Cora and Alice from grass and leaves, and covered up the roof with chestnut shoots. Soon, both girls were sleeping soundly in a small corner of the old cabin.

Duncan sat beside them at the ready, but Hawkeye said, "Get some rest. Let Chingachgook be the eyes for tonight."

Duncan started to say no, but Hawkeye insisted. Soon, everyone but Chingachgook closed their eyes. Chingachgook sat up straight and did not move a muscle. He saw and heard everything: an owl, a whip-poor-will, even the small critters running about on the forest floor.

At last, Chingachgook shook Duncan's shoulder and said quietly, "It's time to go."

Duncan nodded. "I'll wake Cora, Alice, and David."

"We're already up," Alice said sweetly, "and we're ready to go."

"I didn't want to fall asleep," Duncan said. "After leading you into so much danger, I swore to myself that I would not truly rest until you were safe."

Alice smiled and said, "You are a good man, Duncan. Thank you."

"Shhh!" Hawkeye said. "The Mohicans hear something."

Duncan crept forward with Hawkeye to see what was happening.

"I see the tracks of a man!" Hawkeye said. "It's Magua! He must have found our trail."

Hawkeye ordered Duncan to put the horses in the old cabin. They would have to take cover there.

Within minutes, the group was crouched and hiding inside. They heard voices outside. Duncan, Hawkeye, and the Mohicans gazed through the slats in the cabin walls and saw twenty Hurons standing around talking. Branches cracked as they moved around the cabin.

Just as they were about to come into the house, the Hurons stopped. They had seen the signs of the earlier battle! There were scars on the trees from tomahawk strikes, broken arrows, and marks where bullets had hit the ground. Magua and his men were frightened by what they saw and quickly retreated.

Soon, the only thing that could be heard was

the sound of their footsteps moving farther away from the cabin. Hawkeye waited until it was safe and then led the group outside.

No one said a word as they made their escape. Finally they came to the banks of a small stream. Hawkeye took off his moccasins and motioned for Duncan and David to do the same. They stepped into the water and walked along the bed of the brook, leaving no trail at all. They led the girls on their horses silently through the water, covering their tracks as soon as they stepped back onto the hard ground.

The path they took now led them into the mountains. Hawkeye stopped and said, "There could be an entire army of men just beyond here, if the French have advanced as I think they would."

"Are we close to Fort William Henry?" Duncan asked.

"We are still a long, weary distance away," Hawkeye responded.

"We need to hurry," Duncan said. "I would imagine the battle between the French and the English will soon be underway. They'll be fighting all around the fort."

"We can't continue in this direction, then. We don't want to walk into the middle of a battle," Hawkeye said. "We need to go through the mountains and come up from the other direction."

Duncan nodded in agreement, and the party was soon on its way. They moved slowly. It was dark and the path was rocky. A winding road took them up through the hills. At last, daylight broke through the darkness.

Hawkeye took hold of the horses and helped Cora and Alice down. Then he let the animals go, telling them to be safe and eat well.

"Have we no more use for them?" Duncan asked.

"Look for yourself," Hawkeye said. "We can see Montcalm's camp from here."

They were standing on a hill about a thousand feet above the camp. From there they could see Fort William Henry in the distance. Around the fort were fires from Montcalm's soldiers, white tents, and military supplies. "The woods are full of Montcalm's Indians. We may be too late to make a safe passage into the fort," Hawkeye said. "They'll capture us for sure."

"But we must at least try," Cora said. "We must get to Fort William Henry."

Hawkeye nodded. "We can use the fog for cover, but we need to hurry!"

The group raced down the mountain that it had taken them so long to climb. They reached the meadow and started up the path, but Hawkeye thought it might be too dangerous to keep going. Finally Duncan convinced him that they must move forward.

"Stay close to one another," Hawkeye said, "so you don't get lost in the fog."

Just then they heard a giant cannon blast coming from Fort William Henry. The ground shook beneath their feet. Uncas motioned in the direction the sound had come from, and he and Hawkeye spoke for a moment.

"Uncas has an idea. The English cannon has made a groove in the earth. It's deep enough for us to hide in, and it will lead us right to the fort. Quickly, get in while the fog is still thick."

Duncan gave Alice's hand a squeeze as they crouched and followed the fresh path.

The smoke from the battle hid the group as they slowly made their way toward the fort. But it didn't take long for the smoke to clear. They were still yards from the wooden walls of the fort when the fog lifted and their figures were revealed.

After what felt like forever, they finally reached the front gates.

Alice pounded on the door. "Let us in! We are Alice and Cora Munro. Let us in!"

The door to the fort creaked open and they ran inside. Their father, with his white hair and gigantic frame, rushed toward them.

"You have arrived safely! Oh, my girls, it is good to see you."

CHAPTER 10

The Battle Rages

❧

The soldiers at Fort William Henry were brave, but they were also in trouble. Montcalm's men were everywhere: in the forests, around the camp, and near the water. General Munro had sent word to Webb and the soldiers of Fort Edward to send reinforcements—but they were still nowhere to be found. The general feared the worst, especially after he learned that the troops had been sent out to fight Montcalm at the same time that Cora and Alice had left. Anything could have happened to them.

Duncan had been fighting for four days. Now he was standing in a lookout tower next to the lake. The shooting had temporarily stopped and both sides were taking a rest. Duncan looked across the river and saw a French officer leading Hawkeye to the fort. The scout was clearly not happy to have been caught.

As Duncan climbed down from the tower, he saw Cora and Alice. They looked happy and well-rested, much better than the last time he had seen them!

"Duncan!" Alice said. "We've been expecting you! Why haven't you come to see us?"

Duncan blushed when Alice spoke directly to him. He hadn't seen her in a couple of days, and she looked as beautiful as ever. He stammered for a moment until Cora rescued him.

"What she means to say is thank-you for all that you've done," Cora said. "Our father would also very much like to thank you!"

"I'm on my way to see your father now," Duncan said, "to see where I am to be stationed next. But it was a pleasure to see you both. You look well, Alice."

With that, he smiled and waved as he ran off.

General Munro was waiting for Duncan when he arrived.

"Ah," Munro said, "Duncan, I was just going to call for you. I see the French have caught your guide. What was his name? Hawkeye?"

"Yes, and I did see that, sir," Duncan said.

"Montcalm sent him to us, but kept the letter he was carrying."

"A letter, sir?"

"Yes," Munro answered. "After Hawkeye brought you all back to me with such skill, I employed him to carry a letter to General Webb. Hawkeye was on his way back with the general's reply. But now Montcalm has the letter, which means that he knows what's happened to the soldiers from Fort Edward."

"We are in trouble, sir, if they do not come," Duncan said.

"Yes," Munro agreed. "We most certainly are. Montcalm has offered to meet with me. I'm sending you in my place. I want you to find out what he knows."

Duncan nodded. "I understand, sir, and I will not let you down."

He and General Munro talked for a long while about the meeting. Finally Duncan left the fort.

He carried a white flag with him as a sign of peace, so he could pass into the battlefield and not get hurt.

Duncan entered Commander Montcalm's tent and saw Magua sitting there. He gasped, and then stood tall, just like a soldier should.

Montcalm was a strong and noble-looking

man. "I was expecting General Munro," he said. "But I see that you, too, are an officer."

Duncan bowed and explained that he had been granted permission to talk for General Munro. He and Montcalm spoke for quite a while about the battle.

Finally the general asked, "Are you going to surrender?"

"Have you found our army so easy to defeat these last five days?" Duncan replied. "I'm sure surrender is not necessary."

Montcalm nodded his head at Magua. "He will fight long and hard."

Duncan shivered as he remembered all that it had taken to get to Fort William Henry.

Montcalm asked again, "So, you will surrender?"

"I am afraid not, sir," Duncan answered. "And if you will not give us back the letter intended for

General Munro, you really give us little choice but to continue the fight."

"I understand your position," Commander Montcalm said, "but I want to hear it from General Munro himself."

Duncan nodded and left Montcalm's tent. Under the banner of his white flag, he made his way quickly back to Fort William Henry.

⚬

When he got back to the fort, Duncan went directly to General Munro's home. Cora and Alice were both there and were happy to see him.

"Ah, you've returned," the general said.

"Come on, Alice," Cora said as she stood up. "Let's make our way to the other room."

Duncan nodded as the girls left the room, then he stood in the doorway and waited for Munro to speak. The general stood up and paced about the room. When he finally spoke, he did not ask about Duncan's meeting with Montcalm. Instead, he said, "They are both excellent girls. I know you wanted to speak to me about them, and now you have the chance."

"But the message from Montcalm, sir," Duncan said.

"The troops will come, Duncan. Have hope. I do not need to know just yet what that rascal said. We've got some time—our troops are strong. Now, what say you on the subject of my daughters?"

"I . . . I . . . should—" Duncan stammered.

"Well, get on with it."

"I should be honored to ask for Alice's hand in marriage, sir."

"Alice!" General Munro said as he continued to pace back and forth. "I thought you would ask for Cora's hand, as she's the eldest."

Duncan did not say another word.

"Yes!" General Munro said at last. "Of course, yes, I shall be pleased to call you son!"

"Thank you, sir. That is good news indeed." Duncan smiled.

"Now, what of Montcalm?"

Duncan told the general everything that had happened at his meeting with the commander.

"He still wishes to see me in person, even after you told him we would not surrender?"

"Yes," Duncan answered.

"Then we shall go. Send out a messenger and let them know that we are coming. We must bring extra guards with us, in case it's a trick."

"Yes, sir." Duncan left to get the party ready for another meeting with Montcalm.

Soon he and General Munro were on their way out of the fort. Munro's men drummed his departure, and Montcalm's drummers answered.

Finally the men came face-to-face. They looked

each other up and down, and then Montcalm broke the silence.

"I am happy, General Munro, that you have agreed to see me. We have no need for guards. You are in no danger here. I will dismiss my guards if you will do the same."

Lines of Magua's men stood behind Montcalm.

General Munro nodded and whispered to Duncan, who turned around and ordered, "Have the guards step back!"

The soldiers quickly did as they were told. Magua and his men retreated as well. Munro motioned for Duncan to stand next to him.

Montcalm turned to General Munro. "You have done all you can for England, and now it is time to be reasonable."

General Munro didn't say anything. He let the French general continue. "Would you care to see our camp? We have many loyal troops."

General Munro declined the invitation and

told Montcalm that the English had just as many men who were willing to fight.

"Indeed," General Munro said, "if you look to the Hudson, you may well see General Webb and his men this very day."

Montcalm smiled slyly, and then said, "Here is the letter we took from your scout. You may wish to read this before you make any kind of decision."

General Webb wrote that surrender was all they could do! He could not spare a single soldier to come to their aid. Too many of his own soldiers had fallen already against the French, including the ones he had previously sent to Fort William Henry, and to send more to Munro would mean that Fort Edward might fall. No, Webb said neatly in the letter, they must do as General Montcalm wanted and hasten a speedy surrender. Webb would carry on at Fort Edward but as far as he was concerned, Fort William Henry was already lost.

General Munro's face fell as he whispered to Duncan, "Webb has betrayed us! Not to send the men, I've never heard of anything so cowardly."

"We still have the fort," Duncan whispered. "We can still fight."

"You are right," Munro said. "And I thank you for reminding me of my duty. We will fight to the end."

Montcalm stepped forward. "Before you say anything, will you listen to my terms?"

"What say you?!" Munro shouted. "Do you wish to frighten me with your words? It would take more than a piece of paper taken from a scout!"

Duncan whispered to the general again, who calmed down enough to say, "I apologize, Commander Montcalm. Yes, we will hear you."

"The fort must and will be destroyed," Montcalm said, "but we will allow you and your soldiers safe passage back to England. The only other option is the death of all of your men — for we are stronger and better prepared for a long battle. Do you want to see the fight brought to the door of the fort? Would it not be best to surrender now, under these terms, and return to England to report to your king? I have the treaty here for you to sign, General Munro."

With a heavy heart, the general bowed his head and said, "Very well, General Montcalm. We will agree to your terms and surrender Fort William Henry."

Munro turned to Duncan and said, "Not in all my life would I have ever thought a Frenchman could be so honorable. But I never thought that a fellow general would not come to our aid, either."

With those sad words, Munro signed the paper before him and then marched back to the fort.

Duncan stayed behind to hear the specific terms of the treaty. He returned late in the evening, and it was announced that Munro had signed the treaty. They were to leave the fort the next morning.

CHAPTER 11

Captured!

༺৩༻

The next morning, the men of Fort William Henry lined up outside the walls to march to their ships. Women and children ran back and forth, packing as much as they could carry. Munro stood by with a broken heart.

Duncan saw him and walked over. "What can I do to help, General?"

"My daughters!" he answered.

"Have you made arrangements for them?" Duncan asked.

"Today I am only a soldier," Munro answered.

"All of these men are my children. It's hard for me to worry about Cora and Alice as well. Will you help them, Duncan? I know I can trust you with their lives, especially now that you and Alice are to wed."

Duncan ran to the house to find Cora and Alice ready to leave. Cora was pale, but she held her tears. Alice did not.

"The fort is lost," Cora said. "What will happen to all these people?"

"Cora," Duncan said, "you must think of yourself and Alice now. Your father and I will see to the troops. Please, you need to be safe."

She brushed her cheeks with her handkerchief and said, "We'll be fine. No one would harm the daughters of a general. Besides," she added, "David is with us."

Duncan turned to the musician and said, "David, it's good to see you. You need to be very careful. We may still be in danger. I can hear the

Huron's war drums in the distance. Montcalm may have signed the treaty, but I am sure Magua and his men are still intent upon a fight."

David nodded. "I will stand by. Not to worry, Duncan. The girls are safe with me."

A horn signaled that it was time to leave. French guards were already standing at their posts, and the fort was flying French flags.

"Let's go," Cora said to Alice. "This is no place for us."

The two girls stepped in line, holding on tightly to each other.

Magua and his men were hiding in the woods. They watched as the men and women of the fort marched by. When the time was right, Magua let out a powerful whoop and came running. Munro's men did the best they could to defend themselves, but there were too many of Magua's Hurons. Cora and Alice stood still. They were too scared to move. General Munro galloped away from his daughters to find Montcalm and force him to keep his word about ending the fighting.

David stood in front of the girls. Not knowing what else to do, he started to sing. Magua's men found this so strange that they stopped in their tracks.

But when Magua saw that it was the Munro girls who were being protected, he ran over.

"Come with me and you will live," he said roughly.

"Never!" Cora answered.

Magua did not reply. Instead, he grabbed Alice, who had fainted, and sped away with her.

"No!" Cora shouted, and ran after them. "Leave her! Put her down!"

Cora chased Magua through the forest until they reached the meadow where his horses were. Magua lay Alice down on a horse and pointed at

Cora. She stepped up and held tight to her sister. David, who had run behind Cora the entire way, got on the other horse.

"What are you doing?" Magua shouted at David.

"I will not allow you to just take them. If you kidnap them, I am coming along," he said.

"You understand you are my prisoner," Magua said to him.

"I do."

Magua nodded and led them away into the woods.

The ruins of the fort smoked as five men made their way through the battleground. Munro and Duncan were looking for Alice and Cora. Hawkeye and the Mohicans were there as well. They had been watching from the woods and came as soon as they saw the destruction that Magua's men had caused.

Finally Uncas called over to them—he had found Cora's scarf. Hawkeye and the Mohicans looked more closely at the part of the forest where Uncas had found the scarf.

"Wait," Hawkeye said as Chingachgook pointed to a marking on the ground. Hawkeye showed the other men how the footprints on the ground changed at a certain point. It looked as if one of the girls had been dragged. "They have been taken captive."

Uncas came forward again and handed Hawkeye something. "It's the musician's pitch pipe. He must have been captured as well," the scout declared.

"And Alice?" Munro asked.

"I am sure she is with them, even if we have not seen the signs," Hawkeye answered.

General Munro stooped down to look at

Cora's footprints while Hawkeye spoke to Uncas and Chingachgook. The Mohicans went down a different path. Minutes later, Hawkeye heard the elder Mohican shouting.

"They have found Alice's footprint!" he said. "They were put on horses here. They must be on their way to Magua's camp."

Duncan stepped forward and said, "Look here! It's a piece of a necklace that Alice wore." He turned to Hawkeye. "We must leave at once. We must find them."

"Tonight we must make a plan," Hawkeye said. "We'll rest near the fort and start fresh tomorrow."

The other men agreed, and all five started back the way they had come, toward the smoky fort.

As night fell, Duncan stood on top of a lookout post and watched the clouds roll by. The lake was calm, but that did nothing to stop him from worrying. The general had found a house that was not too ruined, and he was lying down inside. Down below, the Mohicans were eating a meal of bear's meat.

Their ears still listened and their eyes still looked, but they were more at ease than the young soldier. They spoke in their own language, but Duncan had heard enough of their speech by this time to understand what they were saying.

Hawkeye wanted to pursue Magua by water, but Chingachgook thought it best to go by land. Hawkeye soon convinced the Mohicans that the water would be faster and safer, and they set up everything for tomorrow. Soon after, all four men were sleeping soundly by the fire.

CHAPTER 12

The Chase Begins

⌒ᴼ

The sky was still heavy with stars when Hawkeye woke everyone up. "Let's go," he said. "And be careful. Don't step on anything but stone or wood. That is a trail nothing but a nose can follow! Not like grass, which shows all footprints."

When they reached the sandy shores of the lake, Hawkeye said, "We must be quick to meet the tide, which will wash away all sign of us."

Duncan did not say a word as they paddled away. When they were safely on the water, he said, "With enemies both behind and in front of us, it's sure to be dangerous."

Hawkeye smiled. "If we can stay ahead of them, we might have a chance."

Chingachgook and Uncas led the canoe through small streams and between little islands. They traveled for some time, until Uncas lifted up his paddle and pointed it toward the forest.

"I don't see anything!" Duncan said.

"Look carefully," Hawkeye whispered. "There is smoke near that fog. Someone has lit a fire."

"Well, let's go," Duncan said. "There can't be that many of them. What if they have Cora and Alice?"

"There is no way to tell from that fire how many men are over there," Hawkeye said. "We don't want to rush into anything. We could land the canoe and go up through the mountains. What do you think, Uncas?"

The younger Mohican did not reply. Instead,

he dipped his paddle deep into the water. Hawkeye knew this was his answer: they moved faster and faster to shore.

"There!" Hawkeye said. "They've got two canoes to go with that smoke." He pointed to the brush, where two canoes were concealed.

"We've found them!" Duncan shouted.

Just then, they heard a loud whoop. Someone had seen them! Men on the shore jumped into their canoes and started to chase Duncan and the others.

Uncas and Chingachgook paddled with all their might.

"Keep them at that distance," Hawkeye said. "There is no way they can catch up then."

Just as they had almost outrun the other canoes, Uncas shouted. Another canoe was approaching them from a different direction. Hawkeye picked up his paddle and plunged it into the water.

"Make for the rocks," General Munro shouted. "We can fight them on land!"

It was a race of speed: who could make it to shore faster? The Hurons were gaining on them. The closer they came, the harder Uncas, Chingachgook, and Hawkeye pushed their paddles into the water. The lake grew wider. Finally the distance between their canoe and that of their enemies grew larger. They pressed hard toward land.

But instead of landing on the western shore of the island, Hawkeye steered the canoe away. The other canoes had given up and turned back, but Hawkeye insisted they keep going. They paddled for many more hours, until they reached a bay close to the north end of the lake. Finally they landed the canoe on the beach, and Hawkeye and Duncan went up on a bluff to look around.

"See," Hawkeye pointed, "over there — that's a canoe. The Hurons will be on our trail the minute it gets dark. They will want to surprise us—to try to catch us off guard."

They climbed back down, and Hawkeye told Uncas and Chingachgook what he had seen. They would have to move quickly. The men picked up their canoe and started walking along a wide trail. They crossed a stream and came to a bit of rocks. Here, Hawkeye, Uncas, and Chingachgook walked carefully backwards to create a false trail.

The men came to another little stream that led to the lake and got back into the canoe. Thick bushes hung on top of them, hiding the men from sight. They paddled until Hawkeye thought it was safe enough to land, and then they rested until it was dark. When the sun set, they pushed back toward the western shore. They hid the canoe on the shore and set off. It was time to find Cora and Alice.

CHAPTER 13

A Surprise by the Water

The land was rugged and the forest thick, but Hawkeye and the Mohicans knew it well. They did not hesitate to run right through the trees, with Duncan and Munro close on their heels. The stars provided direction, and they traveled until Hawkeye thought they should stop.

Dew still clung to the leaves when they woke and began to walk the next morning. After a few miles, Hawkeye slowed down and became more careful. He stopped to look closely at certain trees and always made sure the streams were safe to cross.

"I see no sign of them — which makes me think we've taken the wrong path," he said.

"Oh no," Duncan said. "We've lost so much time. We need to retrace our steps, look more closely."

Finally Uncas found the trail.

"See," Uncas said roughly, "the dark-haired girl stepped here, this is her footprint."

"Magua travels as if he is the French general. They are weighed down by horses, which must be carrying the girls. They stopped here for an instant, maybe for a drink of water, but they left a mark. We have every chance of catching them now," Hawkeye said.

With new hope, the rescue party carried on. Now that Hawkeye had the trail, he didn't let it out of his sight. Rocks, twigs, and branches showed them the way.

But Magua had not made it easy for Hawkeye to track him. Magua had left false trails and made sudden turns and strange footprints. This did not fool Hawkeye or the Mohicans. The horses also left tracks, which were easier to follow.

Uncas left to follow a strange trail and found the animals running wild.

"What does this mean?" Duncan asked.

Hawkeye answered, "They are still alive, but they now travel by foot. We are close to their camp—I can smell it. We heard tell that Magua's people had come to the valleys to hunt for moose. It's dangerous ground, with the French still fighting here. We must find the path they took."

Hawkeye, Uncas, and Chingachgook each looked at a small part of the meadow. They could find no trail. There were footprints leading in all different directions, but they did not make any sense.

"We'll start again at the brook and look closer," Hawkeye said.

The men slowly made their way back to where they had found the original footprint. Not a leaf or a stick was left unturned. Stones were lifted up. Still, they could not find the trail.

Finally Uncas found another small stream that had been covered with leaves. He brushed them away and let out a whoop—there was a moccasin print in the mud.

"Good work," Hawkeye shouted. "It's the print of the singer—it's too big to be anyone else's."

Hawkeye bent down and looked more closely at the mud. "They've made him go first so everyone else could step in his print."

"But there are no signs of Cora and Alice," Duncan cried.

"I bet Magua and his men are carrying them. We'll see a sign of them before many yards go by."

The party walked alongside the little stream for half a mile before coming to a large rock that the water flowed around. Uncas looked carefully at the shore and found a bed of moss with a footprint on it.

"Let's go!" Duncan said. "We've found the path again."

"Now where did they all cross the water?" Hawkeye asked.

Duncan looked around, having learned much from the Mohicans. "Over there — it looks like a wheelbarrow."

"That's it!" Hawkeye said.

The scout walked over to take a close look at the wheelbarrow. Near it he found three sets of moccasin prints and the small steps of Cora and Alice.

"They're fine," Hawkeye said. "They have sure and steady feet."

The group stopped then for a quick rest and

something to eat. The setting sun gave them the encouragement to keep going. They did not want another day to go by without finding Cora and Alice.

They were so close to the Huron camp by this time that following the trail was easy. Before long, Hawkeye slowed down.

"Through the trees, there, is open sky," he said. "We need to be more careful now. Uncas and Chingachgook will go along the stream. I will follow the trail. If anything happens, we'll call three times, like a crow."

The two Mohicans went one way, while Hawkeye, Duncan, and Munro followed the other path. When they got a bit closer, Hawkeye told Munro and Duncan to wait in the thicket.

Suddenly Duncan saw a figure coming toward him, crouching on all fours. He was about to make the crow call but did not want to give himself away.

Hawkeye crept up beside him. "We found their camp, but that's not a Huron. Why, I think it's one of Montcalm's scouts."

"He has no weapons," Duncan said. "And unless he shouts to his fellow scouts, we have nothing to fear."

Much to Duncan's surprise, Hawkeye moved forward and tapped the fellow on the shoulder.

"Well, David," he said, "how are you?"

Duncan was surprised to see that the enemy was, in fact, a friend! He burst out of his hiding place and ran over to the two men. The general followed close on his heels.

"They've given you some funny clothes!" Duncan laughed. "You look just like a Huron!"

Then, suddenly, they heard the sounds of a crow calling. For a second, they thought Uncas and Chingachgook may be in trouble, but then they realized it was an actual bird. It didn't matter. The two Mohicans had heard it as well, and had made their way back to the group.

"What of my daughters?" Munro asked.

"Magua is holding them at his camp," David answered.

"And where is Magua now?" Hawkeye asked.

David replied, "He is out hunting for moose. Tomorrow they are to travel farther into the forest. Then they will go to Canada. They aren't keeping the girls together, though. Alice is with the women of the Huron. Cora is with a different group—across the rocks."

"Why do they let you roam around free?" Hawkeye asked.

"They believe me to be a madman. They do not think I am a danger to them."

"We found your pitch pipe," Hawkeye said. "I imagine you'd like it back." He held out the instrument, which David happily took.

Hawkeye asked him for more information about Cora and Alice. Even the smallest detail could help them find the girls. But David knew very little. Duncan suggested many different ways of saving Cora, but Hawkeye didn't think any of them would work.

"It might be best to let David go back to these people. He can find Cora and Alice and let them know we are coming. When he sees that we can get in with little harm, he can signal. Sir, do you know the call of the whip-poor-will?"

David smiled. "Yes, of course I do."

"Good," Hawkeye said. "That will be your signal. When you hear the call three times, you will come to the bushes—"

"Stop," Duncan said. "I am going with him."

Hawkeye looked at him. "If you do, you will most certainly see your death."

"I can play a madman or a fool and capture their attention. Anything to save Alice and Cora."

Duncan had made up his mind, and nothing Hawkeye could say would change it. "I can go in disguise and rescue Alice while you save Cora. It's decided."

"Fine," Hawkeye said. "Sit down on that rock there, and Chingachgook will help you."

After Duncan was properly dressed, he and Hawkeye talked a bit more. They went over the signals and found a place to meet once Duncan had saved Alice.

As he was leaving, Hawkeye pulled Duncan aside and told him that he would make sure the general was safe before he went to rescue Cora. Chingachgook would stay with him.

"Good luck," Hawkeye said. "You are a brave man, and I respect that."

They shook hands. Then Duncan nodded at David, and the two left the safety of the little bank. Hawkeye watched them go, and then he and Uncas left as well.

CHAPTER 14

A Captured Warrior

Moments later, David led the way to the main lodge. Duncan followed him and did exactly what he did. They each grabbed a sassafras bunch, and David sat down in the corner. But before Duncan could join him, the men in the lodge formed a circle around him.

Someone lit a torch. Duncan could see the faces of the men around him more closely now. Each one looked him up and down, staring at every inch of him. An older, gray-haired man came forward. He spoke in Huron, which Duncan did not understand.

"Does no one speak English?" Duncan asked. When he got no answer, he asked, "Does anyone speak French? The language of Montcalm?"

There was a very long pause.

Finally the gray-haired man said in French, "Montcalm speaks to us in that language. Who are you? Why have you disguised yourself?"

"I have come to see if anyone here is ill. My job is that of a healer. When you meet with men not of your tribe, do you not set aside your buffalo robes so you look more like them?" Duncan asked.

The chief laughed and then applauded. But before he could answer, a low, shrill howl came from the forest. The noise scared Duncan and he jumped. Everyone in the lodge ran outside. They were excited because the warriors had returned home celebrating a victory.

The men pushed and prodded Duncan until he was in the middle of a circle. Flames blazed all around him.

The warriors had captured a man. They pushed him into the circle, too, until he came face-to-face with Duncan. It was Uncas!

Duncan didn't want to risk letting the Hurons know that it was Uncas, so he tried not to look shocked. The women were teasing the Mohican, and the men were laughing at him. It hurt Duncan to see his proud friend treated this way.

One of the warriors pulled Uncas's arm and forced him into the lodge. Duncan was pushed along by the crowd and went inside as well.

Another man, a stranger, stood back from the crowd. For a moment, Duncan was afraid to look at him—he thought it might be Hawkeye, and he couldn't stand to see his friend in danger. But that was not the case. By the way this stranger was dressed and the way he wore his hair, Duncan knew he was a Huron.

The chiefs took their place inside the large, smoky room. The rest of the men and women filled in the spots around them. Uncas stood calmly in front of them all.

The gray-haired chief said to Uncas, "You, stranger, may still prove yourself a man and save your own life. Tonight we give you rest. You may eat. Tomorrow we will decide your fate."

Uncas looked straight at the old man and said, "I have no need for food."

"Two of our young warriors are on the trail of the other scout," the chief continued.

"Your young men will never catch him," Uncas said.

"They caught you," the chief said.

"Ha!" Uncas replied. "Your warrior, Reed-that-Bends, is a coward. He was running away from the battle when he caught me by surprise."

At that, the gray-haired chief walked past Uncas and stood in front of the stranger.

"Reed-that-Bends," he said, "you have brought shame to us. I do not doubt that what this man says is true—you are a coward. Three times you have been called to go into battle and three times you have run away. You are never to been seen here again. Your name has already been forgotten."

The young man stood up and looked at the old chief. His eyes watered as he turned on his heel and left the lodge. He didn't look back.

As the crowd moved out of the lodge to watch Reed-that-Bends leave the village, Uncas crept up beside Duncan.

"Hawkeye and the general are safe. It will take more than this to scare me. Go outside quickly, before they see us talking," he whispered, and gently pushed Duncan toward the door.

The fires outside were dying, as many Huron men and women walked to and fro. Duncan was scared, but he made himself look around the camp for Alice. From hut to hut, he pulled back the blankets and looked inside. He found no trace of her anywhere. Finally he went back to the main lodge to look for David—maybe he could help in the search.

Uncas was still there, but David was nowhere to be seen.

The chief turned to Duncan and said, "You are a medicine man? From the French? Then you can frighten away the spirit that lives in one of our women. She is so ill that we have kept her away from here, with our prisoners in the caves."

"Every spirit is different," Duncan said, secretly pleased to learn where the prisoners were kept. "Some are too strong for me."

"But you will try," the gray-haired chief said.

Before Duncan could say anything, the lodge became noisy again. It was Magua! He had returned. The old chief greeted him happily and said, "My friend! Have you found the moose?"

"We had little luck," Magua said. "Let Reed-that-Bends go—he will soon find the animals. He is the best of our hunters."

A hush fell over the lodge. The eyes of the strongest warriors fell to the ground. The gray-haired chief stood and said, "That name is dead to us. He is forgotten. His name will not be spoken again."

Magua did not say a word, but Duncan could tell he was upset.

The gray-haired chief continued. "The young warriors have caught one of our enemies. See here, he is captured."

The crowd parted to reveal Uncas standing tall and strong. For nearly a minute, he and Magua stared at each other—eye-to-eye. Magua broke away first and said, "This is Uncas, the last of the Mohicans!"

The crowd started to murmur, and Uncas's name soon echoed through the lodge.

"Mohican, you will die," Magua said.

"Not by your weak hand," Uncas replied.

Magua grew angry. He turned to his people and started to speak. He told them the stories of how Uncas had hurt many of his fellow warriors. As he finished, Magua lifted his tomahawk and threw it across the room. It cut off the feathers on Uncas's head!

Duncan leaped to his feet, but Uncas did not move—he stood still and calm, like a stone.

"Take him away!" Magua yelled. "Lock him up for the night."

The young warriors bound Uncas's hands and pulled him out of the lodge. Duncan caught his eye on the way out and knew that all was not lost. Magua soon left as well.

The gray-haired chief walked by and waved for Duncan to follow him.

Instead of walking toward the huts, the chief turned in the other direction — toward the base of a nearby mountain. Just before they reached the path that led to the caves, Duncan stopped.

A large black bear was standing in front of them. It growled and stared at the chief. For an instant, Duncan was afraid the bear would not let them pass, but then it did. It took every inch of courage not to look back, even though he could feel the bear following them. Duncan would have turned around and said something, but just then the chief opened a door made of bark and went inside the cave.

Duncan could now see the bear—it was beside him in the cave! He kept as close as he could to the chief. At last they reached the den.

Duncan was surprised to see David standing by a bed in the middle of the room where a very sick young woman lay. Duncan could see that there was nothing he could do to save her. David started to sing a sweet song. Sitting in the corner, the bear hummed and grunted, it seemed, with the music. The bear's noises scared David so much that he stopped in the middle of his song and shouted at Duncan, "She expects you to . . . to help her!" With that, he ran out of the cave.

CHAPTER 15

Duncan Meets a Bear

⌒∂

The bear continued to grunt, and then proceeded to roll around the cave floor.

The chief stepped forward and told the other young women caring for the girl to leave.

"Let this brother help you," he said to the sick girl. Then, turning to Duncan, he said, "I leave you here, and trust you will do your best to make her better."

Duncan now found himself alone with the bear and the poor, sick girl. The bear came toward him, shaking all over. Duncan looked around quickly to see if he could run, but there was nowhere to go. The bear shook itself so hard that Duncan didn't know what to do. Then its head came off! It was a costume—underneath the fur was Hawkeye!

"Goodness!" Duncan cried, "What on earth are you doing?"

"I left the general and Chingachgook at the old beaver lodge," Hawkeye said, "where they are safe from the Hurons. Then Uncas and I made our way to the other camp—have you seen him?"

"Yes," Duncan answered. "They captured him. They will kill him tomorrow. It's terrible!"

"Oh, I knew it. That's why I am here. I could never leave him to such a terrible fate."

"What happened?" Duncan asked.

"Uncas moved too far forward for me to follow—he was too quick. Then a scuffle with one of the Hurons, a coward who ran away from the fighting, led Uncas into an ambush!"

"He has paid dearly for his speed," Duncan said. "But how did you get this costume?"

Hawkeye laughed. "I came across one of the Hurons dressing up as a bear for a celebration. I tied him up and took the bear suit so I could come find you, and we could save Uncas and Alice."

"Well," Duncan said, "you make a very good bear!"

"One does not live in the woods for so long without learning the way a bear moves," Hawkeye replied. "Any luck finding Alice?"

Duncan shook his head. "I have searched all of the lodges in the village and have seen no sign of her. I was hoping she might be in here."

"You heard David," Hawkeye said. "He said that she expects you."

"I think he was talking about this poor girl," Duncan said, pointing to the girl on the bed.

"Maybe he was, but there's only one way to find out. I will get back into this costume and climb up above to see what I can discover," Hawkeye said as he put the bear's head back on.

Hawkeye climbed up the walls of the cave, just as a bear would. It took him a while, but when he reached the top, he had a good look around.

"Alice is here," he whispered. "There is another door behind you. She is on the other side of it."

Duncan stepped forward.

"I would say something to her," Hawkeye continued, "but I am afraid she will be scared, seeing as I am dressed up like a bear."

The scout laughed. "Of course, you're not much better in your disguise."

"Do I look that frightening?" Duncan asked.

"You could probably scare a wolf," Hawkeye answered. "Look, there's a spring over there. You can wash your face first."

It took only a few minutes for Duncan to shed

his disguise. Then he raced down the passageway to the other door, while Hawkeye looked around the Hurons' secret hideaway for another way out. At last Duncan came to the farthest room and flung open the bark door.

"Duncan!" Alice said.

"Alice!"

"I knew you would come for me!" she said. "But you are all alone?"

Duncan told her that he had come with the Mohicans to rescue her.

"Now," he said, "we need to get out of here— but you'll have to be very strong. Keep thinking of your father, and how happy he will be to see you."

They were speaking quietly when Duncan felt a tap on his shoulder. He turned around and saw Magua standing there!

"What do you want?" Alice said. She folded her arms across her chest. Duncan stepped in front of her and stared at Magua. At first, no one moved. Then Magua stepped around Duncan and locked the door. There would be no escape.

"You can try to keep us against our will," Duncan said, "but we will have our revenge. You will be dead—and by my hand!"

Magua laughed. "Will you be so angry tomorrow when we punish you with Uncas?"

The warrior turned and was about to leave, when a loud growl stopped him. Magua knew that it was a trick—he had seen the bear costume many times before. But when he tried to step around the bear, a louder and even angrier growl greeted him. The bear stood on its back legs and shook its front paws.

"Foolish tricks," Magua said. "Go play with the children."

The bear jumped forward and grabbed Magua. Duncan, acting quickly, grabbed some rope from the cave and tied him up. Magua

pushed and pulled, but it didn't matter. He was bound up tightly in the rope.

Hawkeye quickly took off the bear costume. When Magua saw him, he said, "You!"

"How did he get in?" Hawkeye asked. "I didn't see him." Duncan pointed to the door behind them.

"Bring Alice," Hawkeye continued. "We've got to get going. We'll go out that way and into the forest."

"It's too dangerous!" Duncan said. "And look," he said, pointing at Alice, who had fainted, "she's unwell."

"Wrap her up in those blankets. You'll have to carry her. We don't have any time to waste."

They tried the door that Magua had come in through, but it didn't budge.

"What now?" Duncan asked.

"We'll have to go out the way we came in," Hawkeye said.

"But the chief will be there, wondering about the sick girl."

"You'll have to trick him," Hawkeye said. "I can leave as the bear."

Duncan nodded, and they raced down the passageway that led outside. Hawkeye put his bear head back on and walked outside, where a crowd of people had gathered.

"How is the girl?" the chief called out.

Duncan answered, "I have driven the evil spirits from her. They are now in the walls. But the bear and I must carry her out of here. We need herbs from the woods to help her heal."

"Yes, go," the chief said. "I will go and fight the spirits in the walls."

"No!" Duncan shouted, "Are you willing to have the spirits enter you now? For that's what will happen if you go inside. You must wait here—for the spirits to come out—and then you can fight them."

The chief nodded. "That is very good advice."

The men and women stood by the entrance to the cave and prepared to fight the evil spirits.

Duncan nodded and then started to run away from the group, but he did not go back into the village. Instead, he followed Hawkeye around the huts and into the forest.

The cool night air woke Alice up, and she told Duncan she was well enough to walk on her own. Finally they came to a path and Hawkeye said, "This will lead you to a stream. Take its north side up the mountain and to the Delaware camps. They may take you prisoner, but I am sure that's where they are keeping Cora. We can rescue you once I free Uncas. Go, quickly now."

As Duncan and Alice rushed off down the trail, Duncan turned back and said, "Be safe, Hawkeye. And thank you!"

Hawkeye waved to them and crept back to the village, where he came across a half-built hut.

Thinking it would be a good hiding place, he crawled inside. The scout was very surprised to see David there, sitting on a pile of twigs. When David saw the bear, he screamed.

"David," Hawkeye said. "It's me, Hawkeye."

"H-h-have you turned into a bear?" David asked.

"No, no. It's a costume," Hawkeye said. "Have you seen Uncas?"

"They have him tied up," David answered.

"Can you show me where they are keeping him?" Hawkeye asked.

David nodded.

"Let's go!" Hawkeye said.

The lodge where Uncas was being held was in the middle of the village. In his bear costume, Hawkeye walked right through the middle of the huts, but getting in or out of the lodge would be very hard. The four warriors standing guard saw the bear, but they did not leave. Hawkeye growled, and David stepped forward.

"The bear wishes to see the prisoner."

The guards still didn't move. Hawkeye growled again and waved his arms around.

"Did you not hear me?" David repeated. "The powerful bear would like to see the prisoner."

At last, the four guards let David and Hawkeye enter the lodge. Uncas was in a far corner, with his hands and feet tied up. He stood up as quickly as he could, and pressed his back against the wall. Hawkeye signaled a low whistle, and Uncas understood that it was not a real bear.

"Hawkeye!" he said.

"Cut the ropes," Hawkeye said to David. The singer did so quickly. While David was untying Uncas, Hawkeye shed his bear costume.

"Wait," Uncas said, "How are we going to get out? Wouldn't it be wise to stay as the bear?"

Hawkeye thought for a moment, "Yes. Yes, I will go outside and attract their attention, while you and the musician sneak out the door."

But as Hawkeye picked up the costume, he changed his mind. "No, you go as the bear, Uncas. I will dress up as the musician. David—are you brave enough to stay here and make them think you are Uncas, if only for a moment?"

The musician nodded. "I can, and I will."

When Hawkeye left, he was blowing the pitch pipe and waving his arms in time to his music. Uncas, dressed as the bear, was following closely behind. The warriors paid no attention to them.

Hawkeye and Uncas were already at the edge of the woods when they heard the first shout. "They've found out you're not there, Uncas! Let's go!" Hawkeye said.

They took off their costumes and raced into the woods. When the guards started shouting, over two hundred men ready for battle came running out of their huts and from around the village. Soon everyone knew that Uncas had escaped. The main lodge was full of people wondering what was going to happen next.

A few young men were told to swiftly look around the village. Two of the guards brought David into the lodge. They had also discovered by this time that Duncan had not healed the sick girl, and had found Magua tied up inside the cave.

When all of the warriors had gathered at the main lodge, Magua came forward and spoke. "The Mohican has escaped! Who did this?"

The gray-haired chief said, "It must have been Hawkeye. The warriors are on his trail."

The people of the village shouted in anger. The chief sent more men out to track down Uncas and the scout, while Magua ordered spies to go to the Delaware village and see what they could find out. Runners went in every direction. The rest of the warriors went home to rest— they would be needed soon.

Just before the sun rose, twenty warriors entered Magua's hut. They were ready for battle. Magua stood up and walked outside. Each man fell in line behind him, and the row of men made its way down to the stream.

As Magua and his men walked past the water, they did not notice a beaver looking closely at their movements. It was Chingachgook. From underneath his mask of fur, he watched every step the men took.

CHAPTER 16

Magua's Prisoners

∽

Life went on as usual at the Delaware village that morning. By the time Magua arrived, the sun was bright in the sky. He walked around and greeted everyone warmly. The Delaware chief shook his hand.

"Has my prisoner given you any trouble, Tamenund?" Magua asked.

"She has given us no trouble—she is with the other prisoners." answered the chief.

"Have you had good hunting?"

"Very good, yes."

"I come with gifts," Magua said. He handed over some of the jewelry he had taken from Cora and Alice.

"We thank you. You are welcome here," Tamenund said.

"There is a man among you, one who has been hurting your people," Magua said. "We call him Hawkeye. He may be hiding with the other prisoners."

"Why would he hurt my men?" Tamenund asked.

"Hawkeye has long been an enemy of your people. He kills with no thought to honor," Magua replied.

At that, Tamenund stood up and called out to the villagers, who started to assemble in the main lodge. The great chief told his people the terrible news—that Hawkeye had been hurting their people.

Meanwhile, Cora and Alice huddled together in the group of prisoners. Duncan stood just behind them. Hawkeye had been right. The Delawares had taken them prisoner without harming them. Now the group was surrounded on all sides by Delaware warriors.

Tamenund stepped forward and said, "Which one of you is Hawkeye?"

Neither Duncan nor the scout, who stood nearby, answered. Hawkeye had crept into the camp earlier that morning. Uncas was not there—he was hiding in the woods.

Duncan looked around and saw Magua. He knew at once that the Huron had told Tamenund lies.

"It is me you are looking for," Hawkeye said. "I am the one they call Hawkeye."

"No," Duncan said. "It is me. I might not look like a scout to you—but I assure you, I am Hawkeye."

The chief looked from Duncan to Hawkeye, confused that both had come forward to call themselves Hawkeye.

"Our brother, Magua, says that a snake had crept into this camp." Tamenund turned to Magua and asked, "Which one is Hawkeye?"

Magua pointed to the scout.

"And you believe a wolf like him?" Duncan shouted.

The chief turned to Duncan. "You look more like a soldier than a scout. I can see that clearly now—this man is Hawkeye."

He pointed to the scout standing just behind Duncan. "We will hear what Magua has to say."

Magua stepped up from the crowd. He quickly looked all of the prisoners up and down. Then he began his speech. It was very convincing, but the old chief still wanted to know why Magua was there.

"Justice," he answered. "The Delaware have the prisoners who have harmed my brothers."

Tamenund nodded. "Justice is important. Take your prisoners and go. We need no more of your speeches."

Five of Magua's warriors came out of the crowd and grabbed Duncan, Cora, Hawkeye, and Alice.

"Wait!" Cora shouted, "You are a kind and just chief, Tamenund. Please, do not believe the lies of this man." She threw herself down on her knees. "By letting him take us, you put our lives in great danger."

Tamenund looked kindly at the pretty young woman. "I ask not that you save me," Cora said, "but spare my sister. She is the daughter of an aging father. Do not let this beast take her away from him. Are you not a father? Do you not understand?"

"I am a father of this nation," Tamenund said.

"Then, please, let a member of another tribe speak for us. Maybe he can make you understand the truth before you let Magua take us away."

Tamenund nodded. "Let him come," he said. But the only sound they heard was the wind blowing through the leaves as they waited for Uncas to arrive.

⌒

Moments later, Uncas appeared in the middle of the circle. He walked slowly forward and sat down in front of Tamenund. They spoke together for a long time, but Uncas could not make the old chief understand all that had happened. A scuffle broke out, and some of Tamenund's men accidentally pulled off Uncas's shirt.

The men stopped fighting as soon as they saw

Uncas's tattoo of a small turtle, a symbol of the Mohicans.

"Who are you?" Tamenund asked.

"Uncas, son of Chingachgook."

"It cannot be!" Tamenund said. "Is it really you? The son of the great Mohican, here? Uncas, you must tell us the truth about what happened. We had thought all of your people were lost."

The young warrior nodded. He told the elder man all about Hawkeye, and what a friend he was to him and to his father. Then he told Tamenund about Magua, and the bad things he had done to poor Cora and Alice.

By the end, he had convinced Tamenund to let Duncan, Alice, and Hawkeye go. But Magua refused to leave without Cora. It was a small price to pay, the chief said, if it meant peace.

"No," Hawkeye said and stepped forward. "You may take me instead of the girl."

Magua hesitated for a minute, and then said, "I have no use for you, old scout." He pulled Cora to him and dragged her out of the village. The entire village watched as the two figures disappeared into the forest.

When Magua and Cora were out of sight, Uncas left the circle and went into a lodge to think. Almost an hour later, he came out with a great yell and threw his tomahawk into a tree.

Uncas gave a great speech, and convinced many of the Delaware warriors to fight with him and Hawkeye. He got two of the Delawares' best scouts, and told the rest to wait for his instructions at the camp.

After promising Alice that he would not get hurt, Duncan joined Hawkeye. The small party crept slowly into the forest, careful not to run into Huron spies. They quickly found the Huron camps and were about to shoot when Hawkeye said, "Wait! That is David Gamut, the musician."

As David stumbled toward them, Hawkeye rushed out and helped him to safety.

"What ho?" Hawkeye asked. "How many are there?"

"There are a great many," David answered. "And Magua is there, with Cora. They have left her in a cave."

"In a cave!" Hawkeye said. "There may be a chance we can rescue her yet."

And so Uncas and Hawkeye sat with their heads together, planning how they would attack Magua and his men.

The entire group of Delaware warriors, along with Duncan and David, now made their way through the woods. They came to a little stream, and Hawkeye asked if any of the young warriors knew where it went to. One of them said it led up into the mountains.

"I thought as much," Hawkeye replied. "We'll follow it until we pick up Magua's trail."

Hawkeye took David aside and said, "These are warriors, picked to help us on this journey. I think it might be best if you remained here and stayed safe."

But David said, "I feel in my heart that I need to help Cora. She is kind and good, and I would gladly fight for her."

Hawkeye nodded. "Okay then, let's go."

The men hid behind thick shrubs as they moved along. They crawled on all fours and advanced on their stomachs. They stopped every few minutes to listen to the sounds of the forest. They made it all the way to the river without being spotted.

"There are few living trees here. The beavers

have done their work. We have no cover. We must be careful," Hawkeye said.

He was right—there were beaver dams and little ponds everywhere. Dead trees had fallen all around. They heard a loud crack and ducked.

"Careful, men," Hawkeye whispered.

A loud whoop called through the air—it was a small party of Huron scouts! They had seen Hawkeye and his men and were racing back to their camp.

"Charge!" Hawkeye shouted. And he, his warriors, and Duncan were off. A great fight broke out. Within minutes, it was man against man. Fists flew! Suddenly, out of nowhere, Chingachgook and General Munro were there, fighting alongside them.

The Delaware warriors, along with the English soldiers and the brave Mohicans, were too much for Magua and his broken men. They drew back!

Many of the Delaware warriors were injured,

but they had won the first battle. After a short rest, Hawkeye and his men pressed forward and a second fight took place.

While Chingachgook led a group of men in one direction, Hawkeye and Uncas went in another. They quickly reached the middle of the Huron camp.

Suddenly Uncas saw Magua run away. The Mohican chased after him. Hawkeye watched Uncas run like the wind, and ran after him.

By the time Hawkeye caught up to them, Uncas had fallen. Beside him was poor Cora— Magua had killed them both.

Hawkeye caught sight of Magua as he tried to escape. He chased him, feeling as angry as he had ever felt in his life. Finally, the scout caught up with Magua high on the mountain. They fought, and in one brief second, Hawkeye gained the upper hand. With one final push, he sent Magua over a cliff to his death.

CHAPTER 17

The Last Mohican

Hundreds of ravens flew high above the trees. The people below them were very sad. No songs of triumph were heard on this day. All of the Delaware people stood in a circle in the middle of their village. They were paying their respects to Cora and Uncas.

Chingachgook stood tall. He looked sad, but he was proud of his brave son. David sang a hymn, which echoed through the trees. The general cried openly, and Alice comforted him. Then Duncan led them away. It was finally time to go home.

Chingachgook turned to Hawkeye and said, "I am now alone."

The scout put his hand on the elder Mohican's shoulder. "You are not alone, Chingachgook. Uncas may be gone, but you are not alone."

And the two men bowed their heads together and cried.

What Do *You* Think?
Questions for Discussion

∽

Have you ever been around a toddler who keeps asking the question "Why?" Does your teacher call on you in class with questions from your homework? Do your parents ask you questions about your day at the dinner table? We are always surrounded by questions that need a specific response. But is it possible to have a question with no right answer?

The following questions are about the book you just read. But this is not a quiz! They are designed to help you look at the people, places, and events in the story from different angles. These questions do not have specific answers. Instead, they might make you think of the story in a completely new way.

Think carefully about each question and enjoy discovering more about this classic story.

1. Alice tells Duncan, "I'll have to be braver, like a true Munro, if we're to run into Montcalm." Do you think she actually gets braver as the story progresses? Do you consider yourself a brave person? What is the bravest thing you've ever done?

2. Why do Hawkeye and his friend agree to help Duncan and the girls reach the fort? What would you have done in their situation?

3. Hawkeye tells David that teaching singing is a strange job. Do you agree? What is the weirdest job you can think of? What do you want to be when you grow up?

4. How does David make the girls feel better when they're hiding in the caves? What makes you feel better when you're scared or upset?

5. Magua explains to Cora that he wants revenge because General Munro embarrassed him. Do you think he is right to be angry? Has anyone ever embarrassed you in front of others? What did you do?

6. Superstition plays a very large role in the book. What kinds of spirits are mentioned in the story? Do you believe in ghosts?

7. How is the relationship Uncas has with Chingachgook different than Cora and Alice's relationship with their father? Which one is more like your relationship with your parents?

8. Why does General Munro agree to surrender? What would you have done in his place? Have you ever had to do what someone else wanted you to, even though you didn't agree with it?

9. Why does Hawkeye dress up as the bear? Were you surprised to find out it was him? Have you ever disguised yourself to trick someone?

10. Why does Magua tell Tamenund that Hawkeye has been hurting the Delaware people? Do his lies work? Have you ever lied to get your way? Did it work for you?

Afterword
By Arthur Pober, Ed.D.

༼ ✒ ༽

First impressions are important.

Whether we are meeting new people, going to new places, or picking up a book unknown to us, first impressions count for a lot. They can lead to warm, lasting memories or can make us shy away from any future encounters.

Can you recall your own first impressions and earliest memories of reading the classics?

Do you remember wading through pages and pages of text to prepare for an exam? Or were you the child who hid under the blanket to read with a flashlight, joining forces with Robin Hood to save Maid Marian? Do you remember only how long it took you to read a lengthy novel such as *Little Women*? Or did you become best friends with the March sisters?

Even for a gifted young reader, getting through long chapters with dense language can easily become overwhelming and can obscure the richness of the story and its characters. Reading an abridged, newly crafted version of a classic novel can be the gentle introduction a child needs to explore the characters and story-line without the frustration of difficult vocabulary and complex themes.

Reading an abridged version of a classic novel gives the young reader a sense of independence and the satisfaction of finishing a "grown-up" book. And when a child is engaged with and inspired by a classic story, the tone is set for further exploration of the story's themes, characters, history, and details. As a child's reading skills advance, the desire to tackle the original, unabridged version of the story will naturally emerge.

If made accessible to young readers, these stories can become invaluable tools for understanding themselves in the context of their families and social environments. This is why the Classic Starts series includes questions that stimulate discussion regarding the impact and social relevance of the characters and stories today. These questions can foster lively conversations between children and their parents or teachers. When we look at the issues, values, and standards of past times in terms of how we live now, we can appreciate literature's classic tales in a very personal and engaging way.

Share your love of reading the classics with a young child, and introduce an imaginary world real enough to last a lifetime.

Dr. Arthur Pober, Ed.D.

Dr. Arthur Pober has spent more than twenty years in the fields of early childhood and gifted education. He is the former principal of one of the world's oldest laboratory schools for gifted youngsters, Hunter College Elementary School, and former Director of Magnet Schools for the Gifted and Talented for more than 25,000 youngsters in New York City.

Dr. Pober is a recognized authority in the areas of media and child protection and is currently the U.S. representative to the European Institute for the Media and European Advertising Standards Alliance.

Explore these wonderful stories in our
Classic Starts™ library.